NINJA ASSASSIN

A TIME TRAVEL ADVENTURE

VICTORIA RUSH

VOLUME 6

RILEY'S TIME TRAVEL ADVENTURES - BOOK 6

COPYRIGHT

For the uninhibited...

WANT TO AMP UP YOUR SEX LIFE?

Sign up for my newsletter to receive more free books and other steamy stuff. Discover a hundred different ways to wet your whistle!

Victoria Rush Erotica

1
_____

After her last adventure a hundred years in the future on the planet of Zemius, Riley felt herself tumbling through the time machine portal once again, unsure where she'd land. A few minutes later, she fell onto a soft mat in a dark room surrounded by a group of Asian girls roughly her same age. They appeared to be sleeping, and when one of them shifted restlessly, Riley turned her body to the side to hide her identity. She peered into the inky darkness, trying to discern her whereabouts, but all she could see was the faint outline of the moon through the paper-thin shutters of the room.

Waiting until everyone's breathing returned to normal, she raised herself up off her mat and crept toward the exit door, sliding it open slowly. Peering outside into the empty courtyard, she surveyed the bowed roofs of the surrounding buildings and the immaculately groomed garden trickling water under an arched footbridge. In the distance, soaring mountains loomed over the landscape like giant citadels. Not recognizing any sign of activity, she considered wandering outside to find a place to hide. But she had no idea where she would go or how to support herself, and for the time being at least, the other girls in her impromptu dorm room seemed harmless.

Besides, she was buck naked and white as a sheet in the light of the full moon. Looking around for a place to stash her time machine, she placed it behind a rock in the garden next to the door.

"Where are you going?" one of the girls whispered behind her back in native Japanese.

Riley swung around, and when the girl recognized her Western features, her eyes suddenly widened and she gasped.

"Who are you and how did you get into our academy?" the girl said.

By now the rest of girls had stirred from their sleep and when they noticed the intruder, they leapt from their beds, assuming a defensive martial arts pose.

"Sorry," Riley said in fluent Japanese. "I seem to be lost. I'm not sure how I got here exactly..."

She knew no one would believe her improbable story of traveling through time, but she was happy that her time machine had given her the ability to speak the local language.

"But you're not from around here," the pretty Asian girl said.

"No," Riley said. "I'm from America."

"America?" the girl said, raising her eyebrows. "What in heaven's name brought you all the way up here into the mountains?"

Riley paused for a long moment, unsure how to explain herself while she peered back at the group of girls poised to attack her at the slightest provocation.

"Maybe she's a *rezu*," the tallest girl sneered, running her eyes up and down Riley's naked body. "Trying to spy on us while we're sleeping."

"We should report her to the shihan," another one nodded, glancing toward the tall girl. "He'll know what to do with her."

Seeing Riley trembling in the doorway, the tall girl relaxed her posture and sauntered over to Riley's side, sliding the back of her hand over the side of her exposed breast and down the edge of her bare hip.

"Or perhaps we should show her some special Japanese hospitality before the light comes up," she grinned. "I've heard these Western girls are quite the minx in the sack."

As much as Riley was attracted to the sight of eight Japanese girls dressed in flimsy yakuza pajamas, she felt uncomfortable by the posture of the group slowly closing in around her.

"Please," she said, crossing her hands over her bare crotch. "I meant no harm. I can leave if that is what you wish..."

"In due course," the tall girl smiled, moving her hand over Riley's shaved mound. "But not until we sample your pretty wares–"

Suddenly, the interior door of the room slid open and the tall girl retracted her hand, bowing stiffly toward a middle-aged man wearing an expensive silk robe. The rest of the women quickly followed suit, then the man peered over at Riley, who was still standing awkwardly by the exit door.

"Who is this woman?" he said.

Riley peered at the other girls, and when it became apparent they didn't wish to speak for her, she bowed gently, covering her crotch with her right hand while angling her other arm over her bare breasts.

"My name's Riley, sir," she said. "I seem to have wandered onto your grounds by accident..."

"So it would seem," the man nodded, gazing into her eyes coldly, trying to judge her sincerity. "You look like you're a long way from home."

"Yes," Riley said. "It was a bit of a topsy-turvy journey."

"Do you have family in these parts?" the man said.

"No–I kind of just stumbled into this enclosure."

The man paused for a long moment while he studied Riley's demeanor, then he leaned over to lift a blanket covering one of the tatami mats and gently wrapped it around her body.

"We'll decide what to do with you in the morning," he said. "In the meantime, I expect you girls to extend the proper courtesy to our guest and provide her with whatever comfort she may need."

"Yes, shihan," the tall girl nodded, glancing toward Riley out of the corner of her eyes.

After the man closed the door, the girls peered at one another for a moment then they returned to their tatami mats, pulling the covers back over their bodies.

"You can sleep on my mat tonight," the first girl said to Riley, crouching down beside her pad and pulling her blanket over her shoulders.

"Thank you," Riley said, lying down on the spongy mat and curling into a tight ball, still shaking from her frightening encounter with the other girls. "What's your name?"

"I'm Akiri," the girl said. "It means white jasmine in our language."

"Pleased to meet you," Riley smiled. "Thank you for your kindness. I'm not sure the other girls are quite so happy to see me."

"It's just that they weren't expecting to see a *foreigner.*

We're trained to defend the academy and its occupants from any unwanted intruders."

"What kind of academy is this exactly?" Riley said.

"It's a bujinkan, where we're trained in the art of ninjutsu."

"You're *ninjas*?" Riley said, bulging her eyes.

"Well, we're technically not considered true ninjas until we graduate from the academy," Akiri chuckled.

"How long does that normally take?" Riley asked.

"It depends on when our instructor thinks we're ready. Some of us have been training here since we were toddlers."

"Well I'm pretty sure you could kick *my* ass," Riley smiled. "I've only had rudimentary training in the martial arts, and only since I left college."

"College?"

"It's a different type of academy," Riley nodded. "Where we learn less practical life skills."

"Well, I'll look forward to kicking your ass then," Akiri grinned, peering down at Riley's plump cleavage. "But don't worry, I'll be gentle with your soft Western flesh."

"Mmm," Riley hummed. "I'll look forward to that."

As she felt herself drift off to sleep, she listened to the soft trickling of water in the Japanese garden, wondering what new adventures were in store for her in this strange new world.

2

————————

In the morning, the girls changed into their training outfits, then they headed toward the dining hall for breakfast. Akiri loaned Riley one of her gis, then they followed the rest of the group in single file toward the dining room. When they entered the room, the middle-aged man was already seated at the head of the table, while nine place settings had been carefully arranged with steaming bowls of rice, broiled fish, and miso soup. The women sat cross-legged on soft cushions around the table, then the man clasped his hands in front of his chest, bowing his head as he uttered the word *itadakimasu*.

"Itadakimasu," the rest of the girls repeated while bowing their heads, then the man picked up his chopsticks and nodded for the rest of the group to begin eating.

"Did you sleep well last night?" he said, peering toward Riley.

"Yes, sir," Riley said, fumbling with her chopsticks. She hadn't eaten in over twenty-four hours, and the delicious scent of the miso soup made her stomach growl. "Thank you for allowing me to stay the night and serving me breakfast."

"Of course," the man nodded. "We're always willing to help a traveler in need and welcome new guests. Have you considered where you will go next?"

"I hadn't really thought about it, to be honest," Riley said. "I came a bit empty-handed. Perhaps I can offer my services helping out in the academy with some of the cleaning and cooking?"

The man paused for a moment while he glanced around the table at the other girls, then he smiled.

"You seem to be roughly the same age as my other students," he said. "And by all appearances, fit and strong. You're welcome to join our group and begin training with the others. Room and board will be provided as long as you progress at a suitable pace."

Riley raised her eyebrows, glancing toward Akiri sitting next to her, and the girl nodded back at her with a gentle smile.

"Um, okay..." she said. "But I don't want to be a burden on the others. I expect to earn my keep while I'm a guest in your academy."

"The time will come when you'll be expected to earn your keep," the man nodded. "Assuming you graduate successfully along with the others. The life of a ninja is not without its responsibilities. But let's not worry about these matters at the present moment, let's simply enjoy a hearty meal in preparation for our morning exercises."

"Yes, sir," Riley nodded, raising a chunk of tofu from her soup bowl with her chopsticks.

"If you'll be joining our group as one of the students," the man said. "You may address me from now on as *shihan* or *sensei*,"

"Yes, sensei," Riley nodded, gulping down the succulent bean curd.

AFTER BREAKFAST, the group followed the shihan into the adjoining dojo, where an assortment of martial arts equipment lay carefully arranged on side tables and adorning the walls. Riley was surprised by the variety of material, which included bows and arrow, samurai swords, kendo sticks, and an assortment of other weapons and protective equipment. The women assembled into two equally spaced rows of four, facing the instructor in the middle of the room, while Riley took up a position behind the rest of the group, unsure where she was supposed to stand.

"Shomen ni rei!" the shihan shouted, assuming a stiff stance with his hands extended beside his thighs.

The girls followed suit, then they bent their upper bodies forward ten degrees, uttering the phrase *onegaishimasu*.

"Oh-nay-guy-some-ah," Riley said, trying to mimic the greeting while some of the girls ahead of her giggled.

"In deference to our new student," the shihan said. "We will begin today's class with some kendo practice. But instead of suiting up in full armor, we will practice the basics with light sparring only. Who would like to volunteer to teach our new recruit some of the basic skills?"

The tall girl took one step forward from the front row and nodded her head.

"Very well, Hanako-san," the shihan said.

He lifted two long bamboo poles off one of the tables, handing one each to Hanako and Riley.

"The two of you will spar gently while the rest of the group watches," he said. "The purpose of this exercise is to learn the basics of striking and defending. There will be no blows to the head and light striking only. Understood?"

Hanako glanced at Riley with a slight smirk on her face, then she nodded slowly. Riley simply peered back at the taller girl with her eyes wide as saucers, wondering what the hell she'd gotten herself into. Hanako bowed stiffly at the waist then she took a step back, crouching into a bent-knee stance with her baton arched high over her shoulder. Not knowing what to expect, Riley assumed a similar awkward pose, holding her wand defensively in front of her body. Suddenly, Hanako lurched forward, swinging her baton down hard and striking Riley loudly across her shoulder.

"Ow!" Riley squealed, grabbing her throbbing shoulder with her right hand.

Hanako spun her body around in the opposite direction, slapping her wand against the outside of Riley's exposed thigh and Riley swung her wand angrily in the air, grimacing in pain. Hanako deftly tilted her body to the side, evading Riley's thrust, then she raised her baton over her shoulder, preparing to strike once again.

"Yameru!" the shihan shouted, stepping between the two women and glancing at Hanako with a stern expression.

"Remember, the purpose of this exercise is to teach and learn the basics," he said. "Not to defeat or punish your opponent."

He turned toward Riley and pulled her hands further apart on the handle of the Kendo stick and nodded.

"You'll have better leverage with a wider grip," he said. "Watch your opponent's legs instead of her arms. This way, you will better anticipate where she intends to strike next, and you can prepare to block her blow. Let's try it again, but not with as much force."

When he stepped back, Hanako sneered at Riley as she resumed her crouched position with one foot in front of the other. This time, Riley gripped her wand tightly with both hands, raising it in a diagonal position in front of her chest. When Hanako lurched forward with her right foot, Riley angled her baton in the direction of her encroaching swing, and the two batons slapped together with a loud knock. But just as Riley was beginning to think she was getting the hang of the technique, Hanako suddenly twisted her sword the opposite way, slapping Riley's knuckles with the tip of her wand.

"Ouch!" Riley exclaimed, bending to her knees in pain as she dropped her baton from her burning hands. "What the *fuck*?"

The shihan stepped forward once again, this time raising his arm to signal the end of the exercise and nodding for Hanako to rejoin the rest of the girls kneeling in a straight line at the side of the room.

"You've done well for your first time," the shihan said to Riley, helping her to her feet. "You have good reflexes, and I can see the fire in your eyes. But you must learn to suppress your anger when engaging an opponent in order to channel your energies in the ideal direction. You and I will spar together for the rest of the morning while the rest of the girls pair up and practice on their own time. And there will be no more swearing in this room while you are a student of this academy. You must show respect for both the institution and your opponent at all times. Even in defeat."

"Yes, sensei," Riley said, rubbing her sore hands gently as she nodded in acknowledgement.

3

For the rest of the morning, Riley and the shihan sparred together while the teacher patiently instructed her in the proper manner of movement, striking, and defending. By the time lunchtime rolled around, she felt she was able to keep up with the sensei, although she had no illusions that he was far from pushing his limits. With the sun beginning to stream through the high windows of the dojo, the shihan announced an end to the morning practice, and all the girls lined up in two straight rows in the center of the room. As before, Riley wasn't sure she belonged in the ranks with the other women, so she stood awkwardly behind everyone else.

"You may join the girls in the second line now, Riley," the shihan said, nodding toward Riley. "You've proven yourself capable of holding your own. Please stand next to Akiri-san on her left side."

Riley walked up to the end of the second line and took up a position beside Akiri as the pretty Asian girl smiled at her from the corner of her eyes.

"Mokuso," the shihan murmured, and everybody closed

their eyes to clear their minds and reflect on the lessons of the day.

After a period of silence in the room, the shihan announced *shomen ni rei* once again, and the girls opened their eyes, bowing in unison toward the instructor.

"Onegaishimasu," they chanted, lining up in single file to exit the room, pausing before they passed through the door to bow stiffly once again.

"So what happens now?" Riley said to Akiri after they left the room, reflecting on how every activity in the academy seemed to follow a strict protocol.

"We're expected to shower before our midday meal," Akiri nodded. "After which we'll have a couple of hours to meditate and relax before afternoon practice."

"Good," Riley sighed, still limping from the beating she'd received from Hanako at the beginning of the training. "I could use a few hours to rest and recover from that session."

"It only gets worse from here on," Akiri grinned. "Just wait until we suit up in full armor and we're allowed to strike with complete freedom."

"I can't wait," Riley grunted, rubbing her sore muscles.

WHEN THE WOMEN entered the communal shower room, everyone took off their gis and placed them on hooks on the opposite wall, then they walked up to the shower controls, turning on the warm spray while a light steam began to fill the room. Riley sighed as the water cascaded over her aching muscles, closing her eyes while she felt the sensuous spray jetting against her naked skin.

"I wouldn't get too comfortable pleasuring yourself in the showers," Hanako said, watching Riley's tight ass undulating under the pulsating stream. "It won't be long before I add some *new* welts to that pale body of yours."

"I'll be ready for you next time," Riley said, turning her head to glare at the taller woman standing a few stalls away. "You just caught me unprepared. The sensei has taught me some new skills to better defend myself."

"We'll have to see about that," Hanako said, rubbing her breasts with a bar of soap.

"Don't worry about her," Akiri said, standing next to Riley. "She just likes to bully the other girls, thinking she's the top student."

"Is she?" Riley said.

"Well, the shihan positions all the girls in line from front to back and from right to left, based on his assessment of our skill. So I suppose she is as far as he's concerned. But her biggest weakness is her arrogance. She'll give you an opening if you just wait long enough. She's always so busy attacking, she doesn't know how to defend herself when someone stands up to her."

"Hmm," Riley nodded, turning around to feel the warm spray caressing her back while she rubbed a cleansing bar down the front of her body.

As she peered at the rest of the girls washing their slender, well-toned bodies, she noticed Hanako staring at her bald pussy while she slid a bar of soap slowly between her legs. Riley paused for a moment, twisting her body sensuously under the shower spray while the water trickled over her full breasts and down the crease of her ass, then she turned back around, glancing toward Akiri. Her roommate simply smiled back at her, nodding softly while she batted her eyes under the dripping water falling over her flushed face.

❧

AFTER LUNCH, the girls retired to the courtyard, sitting in small groups in the rock garden to converse quietly among the perfumed flowers. Riley and Akiri found a quiet spot away from the others, and as she surveyed the tranquil scene, Riley was struck by the symbiotic beauty of the natural and man-made objects. From the gentle curvature of the wide-eaved roofs to the immaculate landscaping of the rock garden to the floral pattern of the silk kimonos everyone was wearing, everything seemed so perfectly designed and in complete harmony.

"So how are you finding your stay at our academy so far?" Akiri said, noticing Riley lost in thought.

"It's such a change from what I'm used to," Riley nodded, peering back at her. "Everything is so structured and orderly. I'm used to more chaos and independence back home."

"You mean in America?"

"Yes."

"Isn't that what attracts so many settlers to your land?" Akiri said. "The freedom and space to do as you please?"

"Maybe," Riley said, hoping to learn more about the time period she'd been transported to. "How much do you know about America?"

"Only that it was discovered by Europeans about a hundred years ago, with most of the settlers coming from England. I really don't know much else, other than it stretches on seemingly forever."

"Yes," Riley chuckled, estimating that the present time was somewhere in the mid-1600s based on Akiri's comments. "It is considerably larger than Japan. But your country has a much richer history and culture. There's something to be said for the order and discipline of your people."

Akiri paused for a moment while she peered at the sparkling stream weaving through the garden.

"Not everybody appreciates the strict rules and customs of our culture," Akiri said, cocking her head to one side. "The feudal lords can be quite brutal at times enforcing the collection of taxes. There is considerable tension between our hokage and the ruling government."

"Hokage?"

"He's the highest-ranking ninja in our prefect."

"Even higher than the shihan?"

"The shihan is simply the head of our academy," Akiri nodded. "The hokage is the one who oversees the district and issues orders for the individual ninja."

"Is that what the shihan meant when he said that I'll be expected to earn my keep at some later time?" Riley said, squinting at Akiri.

"Yes. Most of the ninjas are given some kind of assignment upon graduation."

"What kind of assignment?"

"Normally it takes the form of reconnaissance, infiltration, or bodyguard services for higher officials. But I've heard it often takes a more sinister form..."

"Like what?"

Akiri leaned closer to Riley, tilting her head to lower her voice.

"I've heard rumors that sometimes the more accomplished ninja are asked to carry out assassinations."

"Assassinations?" Riley said, flaring her eyes. "Against whom?"

"No one ever knows. That is the way of the ninja. Everything is always held secret. It's part of our mandate to remain clandestine in all things."

"Everything?" Riley said, drifting her focus down toward Akiri's cleavage exposed at the top of her kimono.

"At least insofar as our official assignments," Akiri smiled. "But it's hard to suppress *every* secret among a band of young girls all living under the same roof."

4

L ater that afternoon, the girls returned to the dojo to resume their practice, lining up in two straight rows, facing the front of the room. When the shihan entered, they bowed in unison, offering the greeting *sensei-ni.* The shihan walked to the center of the room then he stood with his hands by his side, uttering the phrase *shomen-ni rei* to signal the official beginning of class.

"Onegaishimasu," the girls chanted in unison, bowing once again.

"Good morning, students," the shihan said. "I hope you found some quiet time to relax during the afternoon break. In this afternoon's session, we will be elevating the intensity of our sparring by putting on protective gear. Please take a moment to suit up."

The women walked over to the side tables where an assortment of padded equipment lay carefully laid out. Riley's eyes bulged at the sinister appearance of the vestments, looking more like something Darth Vader would wear than a martial arts outfit. In addition to the full helmet with black face screen and padded neck flaps, there was a thick breastplate, long padded gloves, and a heavy gladiator skirt straight out of a Roman arena.

At least this should keep me from getting bruised as much as before, Riley thought while she watched the rest of the women suiting up.

When Akiri finished donning her equipment, she helped Riley attach her pieces, then the girls resumed their customary positions in front of the shihan.

"Alright," he nodded. "Now that you're suitably protected, we'll begin sparring in pairs. Because Hanako-san is our most skilled Kendo fighter, she will lead the practice. We will start with the second-in-line, then proceed to the lowest ranked student while the rest of you observe and attempt to learn from the experience of your more advanced partners."

He nodded toward the two girls at the right side of the front line, motioning for the rest of the group to sit at the side of the room.

"Hanako-san and Midori-san, you will spar for three minutes while I tally your points, or until one of you submits."

The two girls moved to the center of the room, posing four feet apart, then they bowed stiffly toward one another.

When the shihan called out the command *hajime*, they each took a defensive step back, raising their kendo swords over their heads. Then Hanako shifted her weight forward, striking Midori hard on the side of her shoulder. The other girl winced in pain, then she staggered back into her defensive position, raising her Kendo stick to the opposite side. Hanako quickly spun around to her unprotected side, slapping her baton against the outside of her knee, and when

Midori's leg buckled, Hanako sliced her sword over the patch of exposed skin between the bottom of her breastplate and the top of her padded skirt. Midori tried to straighten up her stance, but as she started to do so, Hanako thrust forward with her baton held straight in front of her, toppling her opponent onto her back, wincing in pain.

"Kiraku ni," the shihan said, stepping between the two students and nodding softly. "That's four points for Hanako-san, with a decisive knock-out."

Then he nodded toward the rest of the women watching patiently from the side of the room.

"Shinju, it is your turn next," he nodded.

While Hanako proceeded to systematically dispatch each of her opponents with brutal efficiency, Akiri and Riley watched from the sidelines with increasing trepidation, awaiting their turn. But as her heart pounded loudly in her chest, Riley studied Hanako's moves carefully, making note of her recurring patterns and exposed flanks. She noticed that she targeted the small areas of exposed skin under the skirt and next to the breastplate, forcing her opponents to let down their guard before aiming for the head or the chest for the final kill.

When it became Akiri's turn to face Hanako, Riley peered at her with wide eyes, and the other girl cocked her head toward her in resignation, recognizing she would soon to become another one of Hanako's casualties. But Hanako seemed to take special pleasure at inflicting pain on every part of her body before delivering the final blow with a hard slap against the side of her helmet. It took several seconds for Akiri to recover her bearings and as she staggered back to the sideline to take up position with the rest of the girls, Riley glared at Hanako with a renewed anger.

"Riley-san," the shihan said, calling her name. "You'll be the final participant in today's exercise. Please take up position opposite Hanako-san."

More like the last *sacrificial lamb*, she thought to herself while she faced Hanako, noticing a sinister sneer behind her wired face mask. But she could feel her adrenaline pumping, and as she gripped her Kendo baton tightly with both hands, she tried to remember the lessons the shihan had taught her the previous day.

Watch your opponent's feet, not her arms. Shift to the side when she moves forward, to attack her vulnerable side. Never show your pain or reveal your weaknesses.

Hajime, the shihan announced, and Hanako shifted into her customary attack pose with her right foot ahead of her left. When she lunged forward with both feet, Riley was ready for her strike, angling her baton downward to block her strike to her knee. When she spun around, trying to slap Riley's opposite shoulder, she raised her stick just in time to block the blow while both batons slapped loudly against the side of Riley's breastplate. Hanako took a step back to collect her breath, and as she peered at Riley with flaring nostrils through the cage of her face mask, Riley nodded her head, curling one side of her mouth upwards.

Suddenly, Hanako lurched forward with her opposite foot, catching Riley unprepared with a loud smack against the side of her leather neck flaps, causing her muscles to spasm in pain, and when she hesitated for a brief moment, Hanako cracked her baton down hard against the outside of her left shin. While Riley stumbled to her knees, Hanako raised her baton high over her head, preparing to strike the lower student on top of her helmet, but she raised her sword just in time to absorb most of the forward momentum. But now Hanako was standing directly overtop of Riley with her bare legs fully exposed, and Riley swung her sword as hard as she could against Hanako's right ankle, causing her to yelp in pain and stumble backward.

Recognizing a moment of opportunity, she leapt off the floor, raising her baton high in the air and slapping it hard against the side of Hanako's helmet, momentarily stunning her. Seeing that she was temporarily incapacitated, Riley swung her sword quickly around to the other side, striking her opponent equally hard on the other side of her helmet. When the taller girl dropped to her knees with her head spinning, Riley lunged forward, thrusting her baton into the middle of Hanako's breastplate, toppling her onto her back. While she lay on the floor groaning in pain, Riley stepped over her body and placed one foot on top of her sword hand, pointing the tip of her spear over her neck flap and pressing down firmly on her windpipe. She peered back at Riley with frightened eyes, gasping for breath, and the shihan stepped forward, swiping Riley's sword to the side and motioning for her to join the others.

"Yame," he said, offering a hand to help Hanako to her feet. "That's enough practice for today. It appears that some of you have learned your lessons well. It's time for everyone to clean up and prepare for tonight's meal. I will see you all at the usual hour."

While Hanako and Riley faced each other in the required post-sparring position, bowing stiffly toward one another to demonstrate respect for their opponent, Riley couldn't help noticing the scowl on Hanako's face while she gritted her teeth angrily. But when the group lined back up in their usual formation, this time the shihan instructed Riley to move one position to the right in the back row.

Apparently, she'd demonstrated her progress sufficiently well to earn one higher place in the hierarchy of students. As she peered at the huge welt on the side of Hanako's ankle and her heaving torso while the taller girl recovered her senses, Riley knew that she no longer had to fear her threats.

5

After dinner, the group returned to the courtyard to relax and converse in small groups. Riley noticed three girls from the front line sitting with Hanako while the tall girl glared at her from the opposite side of the garden. There was something sinister in the way they kept peering at her, and for a moment she wondered if they were plotting against her.

"Looks like you've made a new enemy," Akiri chuckled, noticing Riley watching Hanako warily.

"It's not like she didn't *already* have it in for me," Riley nodded. "At least now, she'll think twice before trying to beat up on me again."

"That was quite an impressive demonstration you made earlier today," Akiri said. "Are you sure you haven't received any previous martial arts training?"

"Nothing quite as formal as this," Riley said, reflecting on how her fencing practice aboard the pirate ship from the 18th century had given her some useful prior experience.

"Well, if you keep learning at this pace," Akiri said. "You'll be joining the front line in no time."

"And getting one step closer to receiving one of those mysterious assignments," Riley nodded, recalling Akiri's cryptic warning about what lay ahead.

AFTER THE SUN went down and the moon began to rise above the mountains, the girls retired to the communal dorm room to turn in for the night. Riley noticed that Akiri was grunting softly as she lay down on her rice mat, and she rolled over closer toward her to peer into her soft brown eyes.

"Are you still in pain from this afternoon's practice?" she whispered next to her.

"It's nothing I haven't experienced before," Akiri said, massaging her throbbing shoulder under her blanket.

"She really did a number on you," Riley nodded, lifting the blanket a few inches off the floor to peer at her bruises and welts. "Where else does it hurt?"

"A little further down my side," Akiri said.

Riley traced her hand gently down the side of Akiri's torso until she reached her midsection.

"Here?" she whispered softly.

"Lower..." Akiri grinned.

Riley slid her hand slowly over Akiri's belly until she felt the soft tufts of her pubic hair.

"How about *here*?"

"Not so much now," Akiri panted.

Riley rolled off her crunchy mat onto the hardwood floor to conceal her movement from the rest of the girls sleeping nearby, then she threaded her hand between Akiri's legs, feeling the moisture in her slit. When Akiri groaned, Riley pulled herself next to the pretty Asian girl, pressing her finger to her lips.

"Shh," she whispered, moving her face closer toward Akiri's and kissing her gently on the lips. "Move onto the floor where it's not so noisy."

Akiri shuffled her body off her mat next to Riley, then the two women intertwined their legs, kissing softly.

"Mmm," Akiri groaned when she felt Riley press their mounds together.

Riley sucked Akiri's upper lip into her mouth and bit down on it gently, instructing her to stifle her moans lest they wake the rest of the women up. She paused while she listened to the soft breathing of the other girls, and when she was confident that everyone was asleep, she slowly rolled over on top of Akiri, grinding her mound into her bush. Akiri gasped, and as she began to spread her legs apart, Riley tilted her hips, touching their clits together.

Mindful of the proximity of the other women sleeping only inches away, Riley was forced to move slowly against Akiri's pussy while she felt the pleasure beginning to radiate from her hips. As they thrust their tongues deep into each other's mouths, Akiri gripped Riley's flexing buttocks, struggling to control her moans of pleasure. There was something about the act of making love in the darkened room while trying to conceal their illicit tryst from the others that made their interlude all the more arousing. As they began to rock their hips harder together, Riley felt her juices dripping out of her pussy and down the inside of Akiri's thighs onto the cold hardwood floor. While their bodies began to slide softly against the floor, the sound of their skin squeaking on the surface began to escalate, and Riley had to slow down the movement of her hips once again to barely a crawl.

Akiri seemed equally frustrated by their inability to rub

their bodies harder together, and as their mutual pleasure edged ever closer to the tipping point, she dug her fingernails hard into Riley's buttocks while she thrust her tongue into her mouth. By now, Akiri's knees were pulled up all the way to her chest while Riley pressed the edge of her mound down hard onto Akiri's burning clit as the blanket resting overtop of their bodies undulated slowly in the soft moonlight. Riley was thankful a thin layer of clouds obscured the full moon, with the translucent shutters providing a modicum of cover for the nascent lovers.

As she began to feel her climax rapidly encroaching, Riley gripped Akiri's shoulders tighter with her arms, trying to minimize the sound of their slapping bodies on the wet floor. When her orgasm finally washed over her and she began jetting her juices between Akiri's legs, Akiri groaned in her mouth, quivering under her shaking body while she squeezed her ass tightly. For the longest time, the two women held onto each other tightly, savoring their silent orgasm together in the still tranquility of the room.

But soon after, Riley heard another gasp coming from the other side of the room, and as she tilted her head in the direction of the noise, one of the girls suddenly rolled over with her blanket quivering atop her shaking body. Apparently Riley and Akiri weren't the only ones excited by the idea of stimulating themselves in the small enclosed space of the shared dorm room. Whether this was officially sanctioned under the rules of the cloistered academy or it was considered taboo, Riley couldn't be sure. But one thing was for certain. The unspoken tension among the group of ninjitsu students was only likely to escalate from this point forward.

6

For the next several months, Riley continued to train with the other girls, developing her skills in the art of sword, bow and arrow, judo, jujutsu, stealth, and shuriken, steel throwing stars. She was a fast learner and by springtime, she'd advanced in rank second only to Hanako. One day, the shihan took the group into the surrounding forest to test their skills in a more natural setting, carrying an assortment of weapons in a closed canvas bag. When they reached a clearing high on a mountain slope, he rested the sack on the ground, motioning toward a stand of white trees a hundred feet in the distance.

"We've tested your skills in the dojo using a variety of padded targets and cork boards," he said. "But of course, a real ninja will never use his weapons against a cork board. He uses them with a real opponent in a life-and-death situation. Today, we are going to test your skills with a more challenging target."

He reached into the kit bag and pulled out a bow and a quiver of arrows.

"Each of you will be given a bow and three arrows. Your

goal is to strike the largest tree in the distance with as many arrows as you can. We will begin with Akiri-san, then move up through the ranks."

He handed Akiri the bow and three arrows, then he nodded toward the tall birch tree in the distance.

Akiri took aim at the tree and fired each of her arrows toward the stand, missing the thick tree by a few feet in each direction. As each of the girls took their successive turn, their arrows grew closer and closer to the target, with one or two managing to strike it with a loud thud. But with a strong cross-wind blowing up from the valley, nobody managed to land more than one arrow on the designated target.

When it became Riley's turn second-to-last, she adjusted her aim slightly to the right to account for the wind, but her first attempt flung past the tree a few inches to the left. In her next attempt, she pulled the bowstring back even further, and when she released the arrow, it struck the tree on the left side. But when she fired her last arrow, she took longer to steady her aim, and the dart landed squarely in the middle of the tree. When she handed the bow to Hanako to complete the exercise, the taller girl smirked back at her, proceeding to land each of her arrows near the center of the tree, only inches apart.

"Not bad," the shihan nodded, reclaiming the bow and placing it back in the sack. "But you won't always have the luxury of carrying such a prominent weapon everywhere you go. Sometimes you'll have to carry something more easily concealed and from closer quarters."

He reached into the bag and pulled out a handful of sharp metal stars.

"Now we will move closer to the tree and try to strike it with *shuriken*. As before, each of you will be given three chances to hit the target, beginning from lowest to highest rank."

The group marched half the distance to the stand of trees, then the shihan handed three stars to each of the students. Once again, most of them missed the tree, choosing to throw their stars overhead. And once again, the swirling winds drifted their weapons off-target, bouncing them off the adjoining trees or silently into the leaves. When it was Riley's turn, she noted the lesson from the other girls and positioned herself in a sideways stance, gripping her stars with a horizontal grip instead. When she flung them parallel to the ground like a frisbee, they arced through the air, striking the side of the big tree, one inch above the other. Hanako tried to mimic Riley's technique, but this time, only two of her three stars landed on the target.

"That was a little better," the shihan said, raising his bag off the ground and walking with the rest of the group closer toward the edge of the trees.

"Some of you are learning to adapt to your surroundings and adjust your technique based on the changing conditions, which is the hallmark of a successful ninja. But you will not always have the luxury of striking from afar. Sometimes you'll need to engage your opponent in close quarters in hand-to-hand combat. And of course, they will rarely be wearing full body armor as in our practice sessions, so you'll need to make each blow count if you hope to disable your opponent."

He reached into the bag once again and pulled a long katana sword out of its sheath, glistening in the bright overhead sunlight.

"You've practiced with bamboo batons in the dojo, but in actual combat, you will be using *real* swords. This blade is sharp enough to slice through a tree, but you must first learn to wield it properly for maximum efficiency."

He positioned himself in front of a thick birch tree, then he bent his knees and twisted his hips, raising the katana over his shoulder. When he swung his body and sword swiftly in one blinding motion, he sliced the tree cleanly in half, toppling it to his striking side. The girls stared at him with wide eyes, hardly believing that he could cut through a thick tree with so much ease. Then he handed the sword to Akiri, motioning for the rest of the women to stand a few paces further back.

"Your challenge this time will be to slice the trunk clean through with one swipe. You may choose any size tree to attack, but the award will go to the student who topples the thickest one."

"What will be the award?" Akiri said, holding the sword handle tightly with two hands while she appraised the diameter of the surrounding trees.

"You will see soon enough," the shihan nodded softly.

Akiri peered at the stump of the tree that he'd just fallen then she stepped forward to an adjacent tree roughly half its thickness. She raised her sword high over her head in the style of the shihan, then she swung it hard against the tree, creating a loud thud and painful vibrations through the rest of her body. The shihan took the katana from her hands and demonstrated the proper movement, this time in slow motion, emphasizing the synchronized swinging of his hips and shoulders while he swung the sword downward.

"You must use *all* of your body when swinging the sword," he said, peering at the girls. "Not just your arms."

He handed the sword to the next student in line, and she stepped up to the same tree Akiri attempted to fell, pausing to position herself like the shihan. She took a few practice swings then she sliced her sword down rapidly, slicing through enough of the stem to send it toppling slowly away to the opposite side.

"That's a little better," the shihan said. "But remember, the key to using your katana with maximum efficiency is to swing it with a *slicing* motion instead of like a baseball bat. Imagine using it like a saw instead of an axe. Let the sharpness of the blade do your work for you instead of the strength of your muscles."

Each of the girls tried their turn using the katana, toppling trees of progressively thicker widths until only a few remained standing of the same or wider diameter than the shihan's original target. When it became Riley's turn second to last, she approached a tree roughly the same thickness as his, then she crouched into a wide stance, raising her sword high over her head. She knew she'd only have one chance to better the other girls, and as she swiveled her hips slowly with the first few practice swings, she reflected back on the famous equation she'd learned in her introductory physics class at MIT.

$E=mc$ *squared*, she muttered to herself, recounting Einstein's iconic formula. *Speed is twice as important as mass in generating force. Be like Bruce Lee.*

Riley sucked in her breath and tensed every muscle in her body, then she uttered a high-pitched squeal while slicing her sword down rapidly, swiveling her hips as it made contact with the trunk, slicing the tree cleaning in half with barely a sound. When she stood up, the shihan smiled toward her, then he took the sword from her hand, handing it to Hanako.

"Well done, Riley-san," he said. "Now it is up to Hanako-san to see if she can better your performance."

Hanako peered at Riley with a steely expression, then

she surveyed the remaining clump of trees, walking toward one two inches thicker than the one Riley had just dropped. Knowing she had a height and weight advantage over the smaller girl, she assumed it would be easy to break the larger tree, but she made the mistake of trying to muscle it in half instead of slicing through it swiftly. When her katana stopped abruptly against the thick trunk, it landed with a heavy thunk as her body vibrated in pain.

"Alright," the shihan said, stepping forward to pull the sword from the tree and place it back in his bag. "That's enough practice for today. It's time to return to the academy to replenish our energy. We have an important ceremony to look forward to later today when we will be visited by the hokage. There will be no practice this afternoon while you prepare for his visit. We will reconvene in the dojo wearing your customary training gear at sixteen hundred hours."

This time, as the girls lined up in single file behind the shihan to begin the trek downhill, he instructed Riley to take up position ahead of Hanako in the highest rank. As they began to march down the hill, Riley could feel Hanako's eyes burning a hole through her back like a laser through butter. She wasn't sure what kind of ceremony the hokage was preparing to deliver, but she had a sense of foreboding that the easy part of her training was over and the difficult part was only just beginning.

7

A t the designated hour, the girls lined up in the dojo in their appointed positions, kneeling on the floor while they awaited the entrance of the shihan and the hokage. They knew the hokage only visited during important occasions when new graduates were issued their field assignments, and everyone was excited to find out who would be chosen. When the two masters entered the room, the women bowed with their hands in front of their heads on the floor, then the shihan stepped forward to address the group.

"Today is an important milestone in your training, when some of you will graduate and leave the academy. Please join me in welcoming our esteemed hokage, who will be bestowing the honors and meeting with some of you to discuss your next steps."

The shihan turned to face the hokage, bowing stiffly in his direction, after which the women followed suit. Then the hokage stepped forward, carrying six sheathed katana while the shihan knelt at the side of the room.

"This is a very exciting day," the hokage said, addressing

the women. "For a select few, it marks the successful completion of your training and the beginning of a new life as a true ninja. You've trained hard and we have invested considerable time and expense in your training, and now it is time for some of you to begin repaying your debt."

He turned toward the shihan, nodding softly.

"Shihan, who is the first student considered worthy of the honorific title *genin*?"

The shihan turned his head and peered toward Riley sitting at the far right side of the first line, nodding gently toward her.

"Riley-san," he said. "Please rise to accept your honor."

Riley rose from her sitting position then she walked toward the hokage, pausing four feet away, bowing stiffly at the waist.

"Congratulations, Riley-san," the hokage said, lifting one of the swords and withdrawing it from its sheath, then placing it horizontally in her hands. "You've graduated first in your class and will be receiving our most important assignment. We will meet privately after dinner, where I will give you instructions regarding your next steps."

Riley glanced down at the sparking sword emblazoned with Japanese symbols, then she peered up at the hokage, unsure what she'd gotten herself into.

"Arigatou, watashi no hokage," she said, bowing her head to thank him for the honor.

When she returned to her sitting position, each of the other women in the front line also received their awards one at a time, then everyone returned to their dorm room to get dressed for the formal dinner. After everyone changed into their silk kimonos with the six seniors wearing their ceremonial swords at their side, Akiri peered up at Riley with a sad expression.

"I'll be sad to see you leave, Riley-san," she said, tears welling in her eyes. "I don't know when I will see you again."

"What's the matter, Akiri?" Hanako laughed, turning toward the two women. "Are you going to miss sucking your mommy's teat under the covers? Did you think we didn't know what the two of you did while we pretended to sleep? But don't worry, you'll be *my* bitch from now on."

Riley suddenly swung around, retracting her sword from its sheath, waving it threateningly in front of Hanako's face.

"You better be careful where you point that thing," Hanako sneered. "We're not playing with bamboo sticks anymore."

"Exactly," Riley grunted, lowering herself into an attack pose. "If you lay one finger on her, I'll slice you open like a ripe pomegranate."

Hanako placed her right hand over the hilt of her sword, pulling it partially out of its sleeve, then she peered around the room at the rest of the women holding their breath while they awaited her response. Then she cackled softly, pressing her sword back into its sheath as she curled her lips upward in a disdainful smirk.

"You're not even worth *soiling my blade*," the tall girl said, relaxing her pose. "Now that I'm a true ninja, I've got more important enemies to fight."

"I hope you're more successful fighting your opponents than that tree in the mountains," Riley grunted. "It would be a shame to see your pretty head separated from your shoulders."

DURING THE FORMAL dinner that followed, there was a heavy tension in the room while the hokage made small talk with each of the students, congratulating them on their progress and looking forward to the next ceremony when the rest of the group would be expected to graduate. After everyone finished eating, he led Riley into a private room, where he gave her instructions for her first assignment.

"The shihan has high praise for you, Riley-san," the hokage said when they faced each other on soft cushions on the floor.

"Thank you, my *kage*," Riley nodded. "It is only because of his patient and skillful teaching that I have progressed so quickly."

"It is precisely because of this that you have been given a very important assignment that will test your abilities to their fullest. We have arranged for you to take a position as a maid in the household of crown prince Takayori."

"A *maid*, my kage?" Riley said, widening her eyes in surprise.

"It is only a cover for you to gain access to their inner sanctum, where you'll be expected to assassinate him and his entire family."

"Assassinate?" Riley said, feeling her heart suddenly pounding in her chest. "What has he done to deserve such a severe punishment?"

"That is not your concern," the hokage said. "It is simply your duty to carry out the orders of your masters. But as the next in line in the royal line of succession, I can assure you that he will only continue the vicious reign of his father, the shogun. After we cut off the head of the snake, his family's power will soon wither away."

Riley paused for a moment, her mind swimming with a million questions.

"Won't he have some kind of royal guard?" she said, sensing she was being thrown into a lion's den.

"Yes," the hokage said. "He has a sizable retinue of samurai soldiers who are sworn to protect him. But you will have the advantage of stealth and surprise. They won't be expecting an attack from a single maid, especially a foreign girl with no apparent martial arts training."

"How will I smuggle my weapons into the castle?" Riley said, wondering how she'd be expected to overpower a superior force of trained soldiers.

"I've appointed a chunin to provide oversight for you and to be your primary point of contact. He will meet with you every fortnight at a designated safe place and stow your weapons in a hidden location within the castle. If you need anything, he will provide whatever support you need."

"But I'll be expected to kill the prince and his entire family entirely by *myself*?" Riley said, shaking her head.

"Yes," the hokage nodded. "You simply need to gain their confidence then strike at the appropriate time. But you will only have two months to complete your assignment."

"What if I fail?" Riley said, pinching her eyebrows together.

"Then we will send in another team to finish the mission. But you will not want to fail, because doing so will not only mean the certain death of your quarry, but for yourself also. There is no place in our ranks for an incompetent ninja."

Riley stared at the hokage dumbfounded while his cautionary words rung in her head like a booming bell tower.

"Yes, master," she nodded, realizing that she'd walked into a predicament from which there was no chance of escape.

8

The following day, Riley was transported to the castle of the crown prince, where she was granted an audience with his chief of staff on the recommendation of the local lord. She was escorted to his private office, where she was subjected to a thorough interview.

"You've received high praise from the daimyo," the chief of staff said upon meeting her.

"Thank you, sir," Riley said, thinking the less information she volunteered, the better.

"Why do you wish to serve in the imperial household?"

"It would be my supreme honor to serve the esteemed prince," Riley nodded, following the script her handlers had trained her to follow.

"Who are your parents?" the man inquired, squinting at Riley's Western features suspiciously.

"I'm an orphan," Riley said. "My parents abandoned me when I was a small child."

"And who raised you after that?"

"I was fortunate to be adopted by a caring family from

the Tokaido prefecture," Riley said, struggling to remember the details of her cover story.

"How do they feel about your working so far from home?"

"We are of modest means," Riley said. "They are honored to have me serving the crown prince."

The chief of staff paused while he appraised Riley's demeanor, looking for any sign of deception.

"What prior training have you received as a maid?"

"Only that which my mother provided as the eldest daughter in our household. But I'm a fast learner, and eager to please. I assure you that I am just as capable as any Japanese girl."

"Mm-hmm," the chief of staff nodded pensively. "We've never had a Westerner work so closely with the royal family before. You'll need to keep a low profile and maintain minimum contact with family members. The supreme commander is extremely suspicious of foreigners, even those who've been raised internally."

"Yes, santo-cho," Riley nodded. "I will perform my duties faithfully and remain in my quarters when otherwise not engaged."

"Very well," the chief of staff said, standing up and motioning for his assistant to escort Riley out of his office. "You'll have a probationary period of three months to prove your merit, after which we will review your progress. Our head housekeeper will provide further instruction regarding your initial duties. Please follow my valet to your servant quarters."

"Thank you," Riley said, bowing politely before exiting the room with the valet.

While Riley followed the valet through the imposing hallways of the enormous palace, she peered at the huge paintings and frescoes overlooking the immaculately land-scaped gardens and the large moat encircling the grounds. As she pretended to be awed by the majestic beauty of the castle, she made careful note of the number of soldiers guarding the main entrances and the phalanx of archers standing watch on the ramparts for any sign of interlopers.

This could be even more difficult than I imagined, she thought to herself. *It's going to be hard enough getting close to the royal family, let alone finding a safe way out of here after I've done the deed.*

AFTER THE VALET escorted Riley to her servant quarters, she unpacked her belongings then lay down on the small cot in her room, awaiting further instructions. About a half hour later, a heavy-set woman stuck her head into her room, clearing her throat to get Riley's attention.

"Yes, ma'am," Riley said, hopping off her bed and standing stiffly at attention.

"You may address me as *kasefucho*," the woman growled, squinting at Riley's Western features disapprovingly. "I have no idea how you managed to get a job in the royal house-hold, but I will be overseeing your duties. Please follow me."

"Yes, ma'am," Riley said. "I mean *kasefucho*."

Riley followed the headmistress up to the second floor, where she opened the door of a linen closet, handing her a bundle of linens.

"I assume you know how to change a bed?" the woman said.

"Yes, ma'am, er, kasefucho," Riley said, trying to keep track of all the strange Japanese titles.

"I'll inspect your handiwork after completion," the

woman said. "There should be no wrinkles on either the upper or bottom surfaces, and an equal distribution of the material on all sides of the bed. You will begin with Princess Sakura's room. She's normally outside receiving her riding lessons at this time of day. You'll find her room at the far end of the hall on the left. Knock softly before entering, in case she's otherwise occupied."

"Yes, kasefucho," Riley nodded, sniffing the scented aroma of the freshly laundered bed linens.

When she reached the end of the hall, the princess's door was slightly ajar, and she could hear some muffled noises coming from the other side of the room. Not wishing to barge in on the princess, Riley tapped lightly on the heavy door, barely making a sound on the thick oak paneling. Pressing the door open a few more inches, she noticed the shadow of a moving figure projected on the far wall of the room opposite the open windows. Fearing a reprimand for failing to complete her first assignment, she poked her head through the narrow gap, preparing to ask the princess if she wished to be interrupted.

But what she saw next took her breath away, dropping her mouth open while she stared at the rumpled bed linens where the naked princess lay on her stomach with her knees spread far apart, flexing her buttocks while she humped her hand pressed against her dripping pussy. Paralyzed by a mixture of embarrassment and excitement, Riley stood at the entrance with bulging eyes, feeling her pussy dripping a cascade of juices down the inside of her thighs while she watched the erotic performance unfolding on the bed.

She knew that she should withdraw from the room and return at a more convenient time, but the spectacle of the beautiful girl in the throes of passion had her paralyzed.

The princess's figure was the most exquisite she'd ever seen, with perfectly round buttock cheeks, a pretty pink pussy and a tight pucker that kept winking at her while the princess bounced her ass up and down on the mattress. With her flushed face turned in the opposite direction and her mouth yawning open in mounting pleasure, Riley couldn't have torn herself away if she wanted to.

As the girl approached an obvious climax, Riley became afraid that someone else might hear her, and she unconsciously leaned against the back of the door, clicking it shut. The girl suddenly raised her head, swinging it in Riley's direction, and when she saw the Western girl standing by the door, she sat up quickly, pulling the bed sheets over her flushing bosom.

"Who are you?" the princess panted, staring at Riley with wide eyes.

"I'm the new maid," Riley said, crossing her legs to hide the streaks of lubrication staining the inside of her nylon stockings.

"A maid?" the princess said, still shocked by the surprise interruption. "I've never seen a maid like *you* before."

"I'm not from around here," Riley nodded, unsure how to explain her unusual appearance. "I was referred to the santo-cho by the daimyo of my prefecture."

"But you're *English,*" the princess said, peering at Riley's blond hair and blue eyes.

"American, actually," Riley said. "It's a bit of a long story..."

The princess paused for a moment while she regained her senses, then she sat up straighter in the bed, running her eyes up and down Riley's statuesque figure.

"I hope you won't tell my father what you saw here today," she said.

"Of course not," Riley said. "It's perfectly natural. I mean, to touch yourself. Everyone does it–at least when they don't have access to a partner."

"Yes," the princess frowned. "My father expects me to remain chaste until I'm married off to one of his nobles. God knows how long that might be."

"I can't imagine it will be very long," Riley smiled. "For someone as beautiful and sexy as you."

"Really?" the princess said, lowering her bed sheets a few inches to reveal the top of her upturned breasts. "I heard that Western girls are even prettier than Japanese women. If you're any indication, I can see that they weren't exaggerating."

"That's very kind of you, princess," Riley nodded, reaching around behind her to unlatch the door. "I apologize for the intrusion. I'll return at a later time when you're not so busy..."

"Wait," the princess said, lowering her bed covers and tapping the mattress beside her. "I hardly ever get a chance to socialize with girls my own age, least of all ones as pretty and exotic as you. Can you stay a little longer? I'd love to learn how you found your way to Japan and more about your home country."

"Are you sure?" Riley hesitated. "I don't want to get into any trouble with the headmistress. It's only my first day."

"It looks like we're *both* experiencing a few firsts today," the princess smiled. "This is the first time anyone has ever seen me have sex before, and you're the first Westerner I've seen in the flesh."

Riley paused while she soaked up the princess's naked body, then she placed the fresh bed linens on a nearby table, walking slowly over to the four-poster bed, feeling her wet pussy rubbing against her tight stockings while the two women gazed into each other's eyes.

"Well, you haven't quite seen me in the *flesh* yet," Riley grinned. "But I'm happy to accommodate the princess's wish, if that is your desire."

———

9

"What's your name?" the princess said when Riley sat beside her.

"Riley."

"Mine's Sakura, although you should probably address me as Princess or Your Highness when you see me in public. You know, protocol and all that."

"Yes," Riley chuckled. "I'm starting to get used to all these Japanese honorifics. Even the head *housekeeper* has a special title."

"Our country is steeped in a long tradition of reflecting one's rank based on their title," the princess nodded. "What about in *your* country? Do you have princes and princesses also?"

Riley paused for a moment, wondering how much information she should volunteer about her native country. She was still working undercover, and she knew if she disclosed too much, it might blow her disguise.

"I don't know much about it to be honest," she said, sticking to her script. "I was lost at sea at a very young age and adopted by a Japanese family. But from what I've heard, it's still an English colony, so the British king is officially the head of state."

"What happened to your birth parents?" the princess said.

"I can only assume they drowned in the shipwreck. I never heard from them again."

"I'm sorry to hear that," Sakura said, peering at Riley's soiled stockings.

"It's okay," Riley said. "I had a happy childhood and I've grown accustomed to the Japanese culture."

"Are your adoptive parents as restrictive as mine when it comes to socializing with other people your same age? Have you even been *kissed* by a boy?"

"No," Riley said, recognizing an opportunity to get closer to the princess. "But I've been kissed by a girl."

"A *girl*?" the princess said, widening her eyes. "Doesn't that feel a bit odd?"

"I imagine it feels pretty much the same as kissing a boy, but without all the worry about getting pregnant and all that."

"Have you had *sex* with one also?" the princess said, raising her eyebrows.

"Of course," Riley grinned. "It's a lot more fun than doing it by yourself."

"But how do you do it without a *penis*? Does it still feel pleasurable?"

"Extremely," Riley nodded. "You don't need penetration to enjoy sex, as you seem to have discovered. There are literally a hundred ways two women can stimulate each other to experience pleasure."

"Can you show me? I've never been with another woman like that before."

"Are you sure?" Riley said. "I was told to minimize

contact with members of the royal family, and I've already overstepped my bounds just talking with you."

"No one will know as long as we stay behind closed doors," Sakura smiled.

"What about the *kasefucho*?" Riley said. "She'll probably start looking for me if I don't return from changing your linens soon."

"I'll tell her I sent you to my brother's chamber when I wasn't feeling well," the princess said. "Perhaps we could just start with a kiss..."

"Where would you like it?" Riley said, raising an eyebrow.

"You mean, where on my *body*?"

"Exactly. A mouth feels a whole lot better than your fingers when administered in the proper manner."

"Yes," the princess sighed, lowering her covers all the way to expose her breasts and the dark muff between her legs. "Kiss me *everywhere*. I want to see what it feels like to be made love to by another woman."

Riley smiled as she shuffled closer to the princess, then she kissed her gently on the side of her mouth. She nibbled on her lower lip, sliding the tip of her tongue along the crease while brushing her fingers down the length of her spine. Sakura moaned, and Riley angled her head, kissing the front of the princess's neck as her chest heaved in anticipation. When Riley's hair brushed against her nipples, the princess arched her back, encouraging her to go lower.

Riley blew softly into Sakura's cleavage and when she slid her tongue over the tips of her breasts, drawing small circles around her areolae, the princess gasped, pulling Riley's head harder against her bosom. Riley sucked each of her nipples into her mouth one at a time, nibbling on them gently while she felt them hardening in her mouth.

"Oh my God," Sakura groaned. "Is it normal to feel this good when a woman's breasts are stimulated like this? This feels almost as good as touching my *gaibu*."

"Yes," Riley said, peering up at the princess. "A woman's nipples have almost as many nerve endings as the clitoris. Some women can even have an orgasm when they're breast-feeding."

"Uhnn," Sakura grunted, rolling her hips sensuously on the bed. "I like the way you kiss me. Show me what *else* you can do with your talented mouth."

"I thought you'd never ask," Riley smiled, pressing Sakura gently down onto the mattress, kissing her stomach softly as she lowered her head toward the princess's dripping slit.

When she reached her bush, she buried her face in the dense fur, inhaling the strong scent of her sex still lingering from her masturbation session. While she swiped her face from side to side, feeling the princess's soft pubic hair tickling her cheek, Sakura slowly spread her legs apart, tilting her hips upward toward Riley's lips. Normally, Riley liked tease her partner by stroking the outside of her folds and licking her vulva before going in for the main prize, but when she felt the princess's burning bulb brush against her lips, she engulfed it like a hungry baby, sucking on it greedily while she pulled the Sakura's thighs upward.

"Watashi *fakku,*" the princess rasped when she felt Riley's warm tongue on her clit. "I'm in tengoku. Don't stop..."

"Mmm," Riley murmured, nodding her head while she flicked her tongue over Sakura's nub, flicking it from side to side while as sucked on it like a lollypop.

The princess placed her hands over the back of Riley's head, curling her fingers into her hair, and as she pulled her head harder against her pussy, her breathing and moans began to escalate in urgency. But just as she was about to pop off with a powerful orgasm, there was a loud knock on her door, and Sakura raised up with a frightened expression.

"Sakura?" a woman's voice called from the other side of the door. "Is everything okay? You missed your riding practice this morning."

Sakura suddenly turned toward Riley with bulging eyes.

"Yes, mother," she called back. "I'm just feeling a little out of sorts."

"May I come in?" her mother said. "Perhaps I can bring you something."

The two girls peered at one another with a terrified expression, realizing they'd both be in a ton of trouble if they were discovered together in a compromising position.

"What do you want me to do?" Riley whispered, shaking her head.

Sakura glanced frantically around the room, then she noticed the door handle beginning to turn.

"There's not enough time," she said. "You'll have to hide under the bed for now. We'll find somewhere safer to finish this later."

"Okay," Riley said, scooting underneath the bed just as Sakura's mother swung open the door.

She paused for a moment when she noticed the ruffled sheets and her daughter lying under the covers with the linens pulled up to her neck.

"Do you have a temperature?" she said, approaching the bed and sitting beside the princess. "You look all flushed."

"I think I'm coming down with something," Sakura nodded. "Do you mind if I stay in bed for the rest of the day?"

Her mother placed her hand over Sakura's forehead

then she flared her nostrils, smelling the redolent scent of sex in the room.

"Of course, sweetheart," she said, realizing her daughter had been taking a few moments to do what most young girls did at a similar age. "Take all the time you need. I'll have the housekeepers bring you some lemon tea in a short while. Hopefully you'll be well enough to join the family for dinner later today. The local daimyo and his handsome samurai son will be joining us."

"Yes, mother," Sakura nodded. "I'm sure I'll be feeling better by then."

When her mother got up to leave the room, she paused next to the door, noticing the fresh bed linens resting on the side table.

"Did the new maid come by earlier?" she said. "Ume said she sent her to change your linens, but she hasn't heard from her in almost an hour."

"Yes," Sakura said, trembling under the covers. "I asked her to leave the linens and come back later."

"Alright," her mother said. "I'll tell her to make up your brother's room instead for now. Let me know if you need anything else."

"I will, thank you, mother."

When her mother closed the door behind her, Sakura bent over the edge of the bed, peering down at Riley curled up under the mattress in a tight ball.

"That was close," Sakura said. "You better get out of here before they wonder what happened to you."

"Yes," Riley said, shuffling out from under the frame. "But when can I see you again? We never quite finished–"

"We'll have to find a safer place next time," Sakura nodded, peering at Riley's wrinkled kimono. "I'll look for you when things calm down a little. But you might want to clean yourself up a bit before you leave. You look almost as disheveled as me."

"Yes," Riley said, swiping her hands over her rumpled uniform, noticing the dark stains on her stockings. "You're not the *only* one who got turned on from our little encounter. Can you point me toward your washroom?"

"First door by the window," Sakura smiled, giving Riley a peck on the cheek.

10

Riley washed the scent of the princess's sex off her face then she pulled off her dripping stockings, placing them at the bottom of the waste bucket. After Sakura checked to make sure the hallway was clear, Riley headed back in the direction of the servant quarters. But about halfway there, she bumped into the head house-keeper, who was carrying a pile of fresh bed linens in her arms.

"Where have you been all this time?" she demanded.

"I–I got lost," Riley stammered. "The princess said she wasn't feeling well, so I left the linens in her room to make the bed later."

The headmistress peered down at Riley's bare ankles, furrowing her brow.

"What happened to your stockings?" she said.

"I tore them on something sharp," Riley said, thinking fast. "So I had to take them off."

"And where were you going now?"

"Back to my room. I wasn't sure what to do next, so I thought it best to keep a low profile until you gave me new instructions."

"You can make up the *prince's* room instead," the house-keeper said, handing Riley the linens. "He's outside taking fencing lessons, so you shouldn't have any further delays. If there are any further irregularities, I'll have to report you to the santo-cho."

"Yes, kasefucho," Riley nodded, heading back upstairs with her heart beating out of her chest.

LATER THAT DAY, Sakura made her way to the main dining room, where she was introduced to the visiting daimyo and his son, bedecked in full samurai regalia. It was obvious that her mother was trying to encourage a courtship, seating the handsome soldier opposite the princess, asking questions about the youth to generate interest from her daughter. But all Sakura could think about the whole time was Riley and how good it felt to feel her warm lips on her gaibu.

When the dinner was finally over and the family bade goodbye to their guests, Sakura took a detour on the way back to her bedroom to pay Riley a visit in the maid quarters. Sneaking in under the cover of darkness, she tapped softly on Riley's closed door, and when Riley opened it, her eyes widened in surprise.

"Sakura!" she said, happy to see the princess again so soon. "How did you get here? Won't you be in trouble if you're found mingling with the servants?"

"I was careful to make sure no one saw me," Sakura nodded. "We should be safe down here as long as no one suspects anything. May I come in?"

"Of course," Riley said, opening the door and latching it

behind the princess. "It's so good to see you again. I've been thinking about you all day."

"Same here," Sakura said. "I could barely sit still over dinner remembering the way you kissed my body."

"And I haven't been able to stop touching myself, remembering the way you looked when I first saw you lying naked on your bed."

Riley knew she was breaking the terms of her agreement with the hokage by becoming emotionally involved with Sakura, but she couldn't help herself. The princess was sexy, gorgeous, and seemingly as innocent as a schoolgirl. Far from imagining the idea of killing her, all she could think about was how much she wanted to tangle their bodies together and kiss her rosebud lips.

"I'm sure we can do better than that," Sakura smiled, stepping forward to kiss Riley softly on the lips. "Like you said earlier, a *mouth* feels a whole lot better than your fingers when administered in the proper manner."

"Mmm," Riley said, pulling the princess toward her bed. "Let me show you something that feels even *better* than my mouth."

The two women pulled off their robes and when Sakura saw Riley's naked body, her eyes flared while a wide smile formed on her lips.

"You're beautiful," Sakura said, stepping forward to squeeze her toned arms. "Where did you get all these muscles? You look as fit as some of the samurai soldiers guarding the castle."

"It must be from lifting all those heavy bed linens," Riley smiled. "Does the *rest* of me look the same as a samurai soldier?"

Sakura paused as she ran her eyes over Riley's voluptuous figure, then she placed her hands over her breasts, juggling them softly.

"Not your *soft* parts, that's for sure," the princess grinned. "Your breasts are bigger than mine and you hardly have any pubic hair."

Sakura lowered her hand down to Riley's mound, running her fingers through her bush, then Riley pushed her down onto the side of the bed, placing one foot on top of the mattress while the princess stared at her dripping pussy.

"Can you teach me how to kiss you down there?" she said, angling her face awkwardly into Riley's crease while she lapped up her juices.

"Just imagine you're kissing my *mouth*," Riley said. "The key is to mix up your technique between licking and sucking. At first, less is more. Women like to be teased before targeting the main focal point. Nibble on my lips and lick my slit to get me in the mood. The more turned on you make me, the stronger the climax."

"Mmm," Sakura said, rolling her head over Riley's wet pussy while she swiped her tongue over her vulva. "I like the taste of your gaibu. It tastes like wagashi."

Riley laughed while she ran her fingers softly through Sakura's hair.

"No one's ever compared my pussy to a piece of *candy* before," she chuckled.

"Am I doing it the right way?" the princess said, glancing up toward Riley's flushed face.

"Yes," Riley grunted, peering down at the girl's face planted between her legs. "Move up higher on my vulva now. Once you get your partner sufficiently warmed up, they like some stimulation on their most sensitive part."

Sakura pulled her face back a few inches to peer at

Riley's glistening pearl, then she encircled it with her lips, sucking on it like a straw.

"Like this?" she said.

"Yes," Riley nodded. "But use your tongue too. Imagine you're licking the inside of a cake bowl, trying to clean every trace of the icing from the edge of the dish."

"Mmm," Sakura said, pressing her face harder into Riley's snatch and circling her tongue over her bulb.

"Oh yes," Riley groaned. "Just like that. Lick my clit with your soft tongue. That feels so good."

As she peered down at Sakura eating her pussy with increasing enthusiasm, Riley felt her orgasm beginning to well up inside her, but she wanted her first climax with her new friend to be a shared one. Besides, she felt bad that their previous rendezvous had been interrupted, and she was eager to feel the princess's quivering body against hers. When she pulled away from Sakura's face, the princess peered up at her with a confused expression.

"Am I not doing it right?" she said.

"Yes," Riley smiled. "It was perfect. I just wanted to us to be *together* the first time we make love. So we can both enjoy the pleasure at the same time."

"Okay..." Sakura said. "How do we do that exactly?"

"Lie down and let me do most of the work," Riley said, pressing the princess softly down onto her mattress.

Then she lay gently on top of her, pressing their bodies together while she kissed Sakura on her lips.

"Guhh," the princess shuddered when she felt Riley's mound grinding against the top of her vulva.

Riley reached down to pull the princess's knees up around her hips, and as she tilted her pelvis forward, their clits touched and Sakura groaned into Riley's mouth.

"Yes, Riley," the princess grunted. "Fuck me with your

pussy. Your gaibu feels so hot. This is even better than when you kissed me between my legs."

"I told you there were over a hundred ways two women could make love," Riley grinned, clutching the sides of Sakura's buttocks and squeezing her cheeks while she rocked her body harder atop the princess.

"I'm going to ogazumu soon if you keep doing that," Sakura grunted. "I can feel it coming..."

"Yes, baby," Riley hissed, feeling her own climax rapidly approaching. The thought of giving the pretty princess her first lesbian orgasm excited her tremendously, but just as they both neared the tipping point, Riley's door suddenly swung open, and Sakura's mother stood in the open frame, clutching Riley's stockings in her hand.

"What is the meaning of all this?" she said, watching her daughter's mouth gaping open on the brink of orgasm.

Riley flipped off Sakura's body, pulling the bed sheets high over their naked figures while the two girls peered back at the older woman with frightened eyes.

"And what are you doing in the *servant's quarters* mingling with the staff?"

Sakura knew there would be no way to explain her actions, having been caught red-handed in the act, so she sat up slowly in the bed, pulling the sheets over her chest.

"This is Riley, my new friend," she said. "Please don't tell father. We just kind of fell into each other the moment we met."

Her mother's gaze swiveled toward Riley, and when she noticed her Western features, she raised her eyebrows in surprise.

"But she's a *foreigner*!" she said.

"She's actually been raised most of her life here in

Japan," Sakura said. "She comes from the Tokaido area and recently took a position as a maid in our household."

"This is highly irregular," her mother said, shaking her head. "You know you're not supposed to mingle with the staff, least of all with a foreigner."

"But I...*love* her," Sakura said, reaching under the covers to squeeze Riley's hand. "Please don't punish her for my indiscretion."

Her mother paused as she peered at the two girls holding each other under the trembling covers. She remembered the feeling when she had a similar experience in her youth, and she was loath to separate the young lovers from her shy daughter.

"Alright," she said, a small smile forming on her lips. "If you two are happy together, I won't interfere for now. Just try to be discreet. I don't want to send the wrong message to the rest of the staff, and who knows how your father will react if he finds out. For now, I'll turn a blind eye to this little affair. But remember to return to your room before the changing of the night guard. We don't need anyone *else* catching you in the act."

"Thank you, mother," Sakura said, placing her palms together in front of her chest and nodding in gratitude.

When her mother closed the door, the two girls peered at one another and giggled, then Riley rolled back on top of the princess, pulling her knees high up around her chest.

11

For the next two weeks, Riley and Sakura continued to see each other every day, with the princess slowly growing bolder about introducing her new friend into her regular activities. Before long, Riley was joining Sakura on horse rides through the forest and assisting her with her archery lessons. When the time came for her appointment with her ninja handler, she almost forgot about the meeting, climbing outside her window at the last minute to meet with him at the edge of the palace grounds.

"You're late," he said upon greeting her.

"I'm sorry," Riley said. "I had to be careful to avoid detection by the guards."

"Have you made progress identifying the location of all the members of the royal family?"

"Yes," Riley said. "I've gained the confidence of the prince's daughter and have been given wide access to the palace grounds."

"Excellent," the genin said. "When will you have a chance to execute your task?"

"I need more time to monitor their movements and find an opportunity to strike when they're all together. It will be easier to avoid detection that way and escape before anyone raises the alarm."

"Very well," the handler nodded. "I've hidden your weapons near the back of the stables. Remember that you only have six more weeks to complete your assignment."

"Yes, genin," Riley nodded.

After her handler departed, Riley circled around toward the stables, locating a duffel bag behind a feeding trough and zipping it open. Inside, she recognized the familiar weapons she'd trained with during the long winter months at the academy: her bow and a quiver of arrows, a pouch containing shuriken throwing stars, a short tanto dagger, and of course, her long katana sword.

Riley peered at the weapons for a long time, feeling conflicted about her assignment, recognizing her duty to her shihan and the hokage, but abhorring the thought of killing her new friend. She'd grown quite close to Sakura over the two weeks they'd been together, and in spite of the shogun's reported maltreatment of his subjects, it seemed unfair to punish the rest of his family for his apparent misdeeds.

As her heart pounded heavily in her chest, her eyes darted over the weapons lying in the case, then she lifted the small tanto knife out of the bag, stuffing it gently under her kimono. She had no idea what she'd do when the opportunity presented itself, but something told her that she needed to prepare for some unexpected surprises.

THE FOLLOWING DAY, she was surprised when Sakura invited her to join the rest of the family for dinner, and before they left to attend the banquet, she hid her tanto knife under the inside sash of her robe. Although it was a modest weapon, she knew that with her extensive ninja training, she'd be able to wield it swiftly to execute the four members of the family if necessary. The hard part would be getting out of the palace before the guards suspected any foul play.

When the two girls entered the dining room, Sakura introduced Riley to the rest of her family, then the five of them knelt down around the sumptuously appointed table.

"Riley," the princess said, nodding toward her father. "This is my father, Prince Takayori. Father, this is my new friend, Riley."

"Pleased to meet you, Riley-san," her father said, nodding his head softly. "I've heard a great deal about you. I'm happy to see that my daughter has found a new friend. I was beginning to worry that we'd never get her out of her room."

"Thank you, your majesty," Riley said, bowing at the waist. "I'm glad to assist the royal household any way I can."

Sakura's brother stifled a laugh, and the princess peered at him with an angry expression.

"And this is my *brother*, Prince Hiroshi."

"Pleased to meet you, your majesty," Riley said, turning and bowing politely toward the prince.

"And you've already met my *mother* of course, Princess Ichiro," Sakura said, smiling toward her mother.

"It's good to see you again, your highness," Riley said, bowing formally.

"Yes," her mother smiled. "I'm happy to see you under less...*clandestine* conditions. I thought it was time to take you out of the shadows, with the two of you becoming such fast friends."

"Thank you," Riley nodded. "I hope I haven't been over-stepping my bounds as a member of the staff."

"Not at all," her father said, motioning for everyone to become seated. "My wife was a commoner also, when we first met. I'm just happy to see my daughter finally opening up around other people."

"Although if she keeps *this* up," Sakura's brother snickered while he ran his eyes over Riley's hourglass figure in her tight kimono. "She won't be able to produce an heir to the throne."

"That's *your* job as my eldest son," the crown prince said, turning toward Hiroshi with a disapproving glance. "And I'll mind you to keep your personal comments to yourself in the presence of our honored guest."

"But she's only a *maid*!" Hiroshi said, squinting his eyes at Riley's blond hair and other Western features.

"That may be true, but she's your sister's companion, and we will respect her choices, just as we've respected your extra-curricular distractions. Now, let us enjoy our meal while we get to know more about our new guest."

There was a long silence while everybody picked up their chopsticks and began eating their food, then the crown prince turned toward Riley and smiled.

"I noticed you and Sakura practicing with bow and arrow in the courtyard the other day," he said. "You seem exceptionally skilled for someone with no formal training. Where did you develop your talent?"

Riley could feel her pulse coursing through her veins while she made note of the two guards standing watch at the exit doors to the dining room. She knew they would be harder to overcome in the heat of the battle, but she was confident that her quick reflexes and superior swordsman-ship would prevail.

"My Japanese father taught me in the forested hills of Tokaido," she said. "We were of modest means, and it was a good way to catch wild game to feed the family."

"That's good to hear," Sakura's father smiled. "I feel far more comfortable knowing my daughter is being protected by a skilled archer."

Riley felt the handle of her dagger digging into the side of her ribs as she kneeled on the floor, reminding her of her commitment to the hokage when she graduated from the academy. She knew it would only take a few moments to dispatch the entire group, but something gave her pause as she peered at the prince and his family.

"Yes," she said, glancing across the table at Sakura's brother, who was still glaring at her suspiciously while he chewed his rice with clenched teeth. "I understand there are some who are unhappy with the current government."

Sakura's mother turned her head suddenly toward Riley, pausing her chopsticks below her mouth, surprised that she'd have the temerity to challenge the crown prince's authority.

"There've been some unfortunate misunderstandings in certain parts of the country," the crown prince nodded. "I haven't always agreed with my father's approach to managing dissent, and I will rule in a more equitable manner when it's my turn to assume the crown."

"I understand there've been rumors of uprisings in your home country as well," Sakura's mother said. "How do you believe the people of America will respond to the King of England's rising levies on their earnings?"

"I know very little about my home country," Riley said. "I was brought to Japan at a young age and raised by a Japanese family. It seems a world away from what I've known my whole life."

"Indeed," the crown prince said. "There is much we can learn from the example set by the settlers of the new world. They seem to be enjoying a freedom and prosperity that those of us in more authoritarian cultures can only dream of."

The more she listened to the prince, the more convinced Riley became that he and his family had little to do with the antipathy the hokage and his community felt toward the ruling emperor. On the contrary, killing him and his family would only embolden his oppressive reign, opening the door for more killing and even higher taxes. As she began to feel the muscles in her body slowly relax, she smiled in the direction of the pretty princess sitting next to her.

The feeling of peace that washed over her confirmed something she'd long been thinking. That she would be unable to go through with the planned killing of the royal family when the chips were down. How she would respond to the likely reaction of her ninja clan was a whole other matter.

Over the next two weeks, Riley carefully scoped out the palace fortifications and guard positions. She was no longer concerned about how she would bypass the defenses to make her escape, rather how secure it might be to another attack. She knew that if she didn't follow through with her promise to execute the royal family that her hokage would send a new team in to finish the task.

By all appearances, the palace battlements looked impenetrable from the outside. With tall stone walls surrounded by a wide moat, plus a full regiment of samurai soldiers guarding every entrance and archers manning the ramparts on every side, it appeared impossible to breach the outer perimeter. But Riley knew if it had been so easy for her to gain access to the inner sanctum using false pretenses, so it would likely be for other spies sent by her handlers. Plus, shinobi were specially trained in the art of stealth and penetration, and once they were inside the castle, they could strike swiftly before anyone suspected any foul play.

She was tempted to tell the prince of her hokage's intentions, but she knew it probably wouldn't make much difference in the end. The ninja would find a way into the castle one way or the other, then it would only be a matter of trying to stop them before they carried out their task. Besides, if she told him that she'd been sent to the castle as a spy to execute his family, she was convinced that he'd separate her from Sakura and lock her in a dungeon. One way or another, the defense of the royal family now rested squarely in her hands. She was the only one who knew the strategies and techniques of the ninja, and she was the only one who could stop them when they decided to attack.

When the time came for her fortnightly update with her handler, she dreaded the thought of meeting him again, knowing that she could no longer pretend to go along with the plan. At the appointed hour, she slipped out of her window and crept up to the edge of the forest, noticing her genin standing by a tree, keeping a close watch for any sign of palace guards. Creeping across the loose undercover the way she'd been trained, spreading her toes apart to avoid stepping on twigs so as not to make any sound, she approached the genin from his rear side until she was only a few feet away.

She could have easily killed him with her tanto, but she knew that would only raise the alarm among her clan even faster, and the less killing she had to do, the better. When the genin felt her warm breath on the back of his neck, he swung around, flaring his eyes angrily.

"Riley!" he said. "Why were you creeping up on me?"

"I didn't want to make any noise and draw the attention of the foot patrols," Riley lied, slipping her tanto back under her robe.

"Do they suspect any sign of foul play?"

"Not that I can tell," Riley said. "Everything is quiet and normal inside the palace."

"Good," the genin said. "What's taking you so long to complete your task? I thought you said you'd gained the confidence of the princess and gotten closer to the rest of the family?"

"Yes," Riley said, hesitating as she exhaled deeply. "But I've been thinking. The prince and his family don't seem to pose any kind of threat. It's his *father* who's responsible for the exploitation of the people. The prince has little or no involvement in the day-to-day affairs of the government."

"That's not for you to judge," the genin said. "Your job is simply to follow through on the orders given by your hokage."

Riley paused while she took a step back to put some more distance between herself and her handler.

"I'm sorry," she said. "But I can't bring myself to do it. These people are innocent of any wrongdoing, and they don't deserve to die."

Riley sensed the outrage in the genin's eyes, and for a brief moment, she thought he might strike out in an attempt to slay her. As she gripped the handle of her dagger tightly under her kimono, he peered at her vacantly for the longest time. Then he relaxed his pose, cocking his head slightly to the side.

"You know what this means of course?" he said.

"Yes," Riley nodded. "I'll be excommunicated from my clan."

"It's much worse than that," the genin said, staring at Riley with steely eyes. "You'll now be considered an enemy on an equal footing with your targets. We will kill these infidels with or without your help. Unfortunately, this time you'll be included among the casualties."

"Tell the hokage I'll be ready," Riley said, crouching into the kokutsu position, preparing to defend herself. "I will defend those who are innocent with all of my strength and power. Don't make the mistake of being on the wrong side of history."

"It is *you* who is making a grave mistake, Riley-san, not I," the genin said. "We will see who appears on the wrong side of history."

13

After her meeting with the genin, Riley doubled back behind the palace stables to retrieve the rest of her weapons. She wasn't sure when she'd need them, but she wanted to be fully prepared when the inevitable happened. She knew the odds would be stacked against her if the hokage sent the full force of his ninja army against her, but at least she'd have the nominal support of the palace guards to assist her if they breached the perimeter. The hard part would be stopping the team before they had a chance to attack the royal family.

Stuffing her katana down the back of her robe and slinging her bow and pouch of shuriken over her shoulders, she crept back to the edge of the servant quarters, sneaking back into the palace through her unlocked window. She was surprised how easy it was to avoid detection from the guards using the stealth techniques she'd learned at the academy, especially under the cover of darkness. Clinging to the narrow cracks between the blocks of masonry on the outside walls, she knew full well that her ninja brethren would use the same techniques when the time came for them to invade the castle.

Later that night, Sakura returned to Riley's room for a late-night rendezvous, noticing a change in Riley's demeanor.

"Is everything alright?" the princess said, feeling the tension in her shoulders and a new sense of aloofness.

"Yes," Riley lied, not wanting to worry the princess about what she'd learned from her handler, knowing there was little more they could do to protect her family. "I've just been a little distracted lately."

"By what?" Sakura said. "Now that our affair is out in the open, we don't have to worry about hiding anymore. My father's given tacit approval for our relationship, and we're insulated from outside meddling in the relative safety of the palace compound."

"It's not that..." Riley said. "I'm more worried about the *future*. Regarding the level of unrest among the peasants, and a possible uprising. History is full of revolutions by the people overthrowing their rulers. Who knows what they might do if they catch a foreigner having an illicit affair with the granddaughter of the emperor."

"You worry too much," Sakura smiled, snuggling up closer to Riley while slipping her hand under her kimono. "Our family has ruled this country peacefully for over a hundred years. Plus, our castle is defended by the best-trained soldiers in all of Japan. No one would dare attack a full regiment of samurai sword to defend their daimyo."

"I suppose so," Riley nodded, turning toward Sakura to kiss her softly on the neck. "There's nothing we can do about it right now anyway, so we might as well embrace the moment."

"Exactly," Sakura said, referring to the Japanese principle

of *ichigo ichie.* "I feel the need for a little personal pleasure right now."

"Mmm," Riley hummed, untying the sash to the princess's robe. "You know, we could just as easily have done this in *your* room, where we've got more room to stretch out."

"Yes, but I don't trust the housekeepers," Sakura said. "After the kasefucho discovered your stockings in my washroom, who knows what other kind of spying she's doing."

"You might be right," Riley nodded, opening the princess's robe and leaning in to suck on her hard nipples. "Somehow it seems more exciting down here anyway."

"Yes," Sakura said, pulling Riley's head against her chest as she arched her back in pleasure. "Show me some more of those *rezubian* techniques that you Western girls practice."

"I think we've already tried most of the ways two women can make love to one another," Riley smiled. "But there was one other technique that I've been dying to try out with you..."

"Mmm," Sakura said, pulling off the rest of her clothes and throwing them toward the foot of the bed. "I'm dripping wet. I want to feel your gaibu rubbing against me."

"Way ahead of you, your majesty," Riley smiled, pulling off her kimono and spreading Sakura's knees apart.

She knelt between the princess's legs, then she pulled her left knee forward, tilting her body partly to the side while she shifted her hips forward, pressing their pussies together.

"Yes, Riley-san," Sakura panted, using the more formal term to address her lover. "Kneel before your princess while you pay homage to her altar."

"And what a pretty temple it *is*," Riley grinned, staring down at her glistening vulva while they ground their pussies together. "I'm gonna squirt all over your royal pussy and show you how the other half lives."

"Yes, my loyal servant," Sakura grunted, continuing their playful role-playing banter. "Soak my pussy with your peasant juices. I want to watch you peeing all over me when you ogazumu."

"I like it when you talk dirty to me," Riley groaned, feeling her pleasure building toward a powerful climax. "I wonder what your father would say if he could hear you now."

"Or my *brother*," Sakura chuckled. "I've noticed the way he stares at you. I think he's just as obsessed about Western women as I am."

"Maybe," Riley grunted. "But I prefer girls. And you're the prettiest girl I've seen in a long time."

Suddenly, Sakura grabbed the side of Riley's hips as her mouth began to gape open.

"I feel it coming," she groaned. "Spray your love juices on my pussy. I want to watch you come with me."

"Fuck yes," Riley hissed, feeling her pussy beginning to contract in the throes of climax. *"Uhnn..."*

"Oh my God," Sakura gasped when she saw Riley's juices jetting out the side of their mashed pussies. "And to think I'd only been dreaming about fucking *boys* before I met you."

While the two women rocked their bodies together on the bouncing bed frame, suddenly there was the sound of something falling onto the floor, and Sakura twisted her head, noticing the edge of a bow poking out under the mattress.

"What the hell is *that*?" she said, sitting up abruptly. "What are you doing with a bow under the bed?"

Riley paused for a moment, peering into Sakura's eyes as she felt her juices dripping down the inside of both their thighs. She thought about making up another improbable story, then she noticed the dark shadow of a ninja-clad figure climbing up the side of the castle outside her window.

"I haven't got time to explain right now," she said, jumping off the bed and retrieving the rest of her equipment attached to the underside of the mattress. "I need you to alert the guards to the intrusion of an assassination squad."

"A *what*?" Sakura said, flaring her eyes open in surprise. "How do you know they mean to kill us?"

"It's a long story," Riley said. "You just have to trust me for now. We haven't got much time. Tell the rest of your family to barricade themselves in their rooms with as many guards as they can muster. Your soldiers aren't the *only* ones trained in the martial arts. There's a whole other society of secret warriors trained to infiltrate and kill those in power."

Sakura paused as she watched Riley tie her kimono belt around her naked waist and insert her katana sword beside her hips, throwing her pouch of shuriken darts over her shoulder and picking up her bow and quiver of arrows while heading toward the door.

"You're not really just a maid from Tokaido, are you?" the princess said.

"Well, I was trained in the Tokaido area," Riley nodded, glancing outside her window to watch a band of ninja soldiers climbing the outside walls of the palace like a swarm of spiders. "But not as a *maid*."

As she silently slipped out the door of her room, the princess peered back at her with a slack jaw, frozen in fear.

14

As Riley rushed upstairs toward the royal chambers, she heard some commotion in the hallway. Rounding a corner, she saw two samurai soldiers standing guard outside the crown prince's bedroom, engaged in a sword fight with two black-clad ninjas. It didn't take long for the ninjas to neutralize the guards, and as they began to open the prince's door, Riley loaded two arrows into her bow, dropping them with pinpoint shots to their hearts. A new swarm of ninjas raced down the hall in her direction, and she picked them off one at a time until her quiver ran dry. Drawing her katana from its sheath, she confronted the three remaining attackers, twisting her body to avoid their blows and felling them with swift slices to their abdomens.

Noticing Sakura's brother's door open at the end of the hall, she raced toward his chamber just in time to catch another ninja holding a katana high over his shoulder, preparing to slice off the prince's head while he stood immobilized in fear. Realizing she couldn't close the distance in time, she reached into her shuriken pouch and flung a steel dart in the direction of the ninja, striking him on the shoulder as he flinched in pain. Twisting around angrily, he lunged at Riley, and she fell to her knees, barely avoiding the swing of his blade over her swirling hair. But when he charged back toward her, this time she was ready, blocking his sideward swing, then raking her sword swiftly upward, slicing open the front of his throat.

While the attacker gasped for air with blood spewing out of his neck, the young prince peered at Riley dumbfounded, staring at her naked body splattered in blood.

"Are you okay?" she said.

He nodded in stunned silence, then she walked toward him, handing him her sword.

"Do you know how to use this?"

"Yes," he said hesitatingly, wondering how the mysterious maid could single-handedly overpower a team of trained ninjas.

"Barricade your door after I leave," Riley said. "If anyone comes in, don't hesitate to kill them. The palace is under attack and I'm not sure how many more assailants there are. Wait here until I return."

The prince nodded slowly, his chest still heaving in fright.

Suddenly, Riley heard a blood-curdling scream coming from the direction of Sakura's chamber, and she darted into the hall, noticing a lone ninja guarding her closed door. With the only weapons she had left being a handful of shuriken stars and the small tanto dagger nestled under her belt, she rushed toward Sakura's bedroom as the guard loaded her bow, firing a succession of arrows in Riley's direction. Tumbling down the hall and shifting from side to side like a linebacker, she managed to avoid the darts until she was within striking distance of the guard. But as she lifted her dagger in front of her chest preparing to slice the ninja's throat, she noticed something familiar in her eyes.

"Akiri?" she said, recognizing her lover from the academy.

"Riley?" Akiri said, barely recognizing her friend under the splatter of blood coating her face and body. "What are you doing here?"

"This was my assignment when I graduated from the academy," Riley nodded. "I was sent here to kill the royal family."

Akiri pinched her eyebrows in confusion, holding her hand stiffly over the hilt of her sword.

"Then why are you fighting us and defending them?" she said.

"I haven't got time to explain right now," Riley said, listening to muffled sounds behind the door. "The hokage was wrong about the prince and his family. These people are innocent of any wrongdoing."

"But what about our *vows*?" Akiri said, darting her eyes over Riley's face, feeling conflicted about what she should do.

"Sometimes you have to do what you know is right in your heart," Riley said. "You're just going to have to trust me for now. I need to get in there to save the princess. Are you with me or against me?"

Akiri paused for a long moment, then she nodded softly, stepping to the side.

"Guard the door in case any more attackers approach the chamber," Riley said, reaching to unlatch the door. "We'll sort all this out later after all the members of the royal family are safely secured."

When she swung open the door to the princess's

bedroom, she saw Hanako standing in the middle of the room holding Sakura with her arm wrapped around her chest and a dagger pressed against the side of her neck.

"Well, if it isn't our old friend, *Riley*," Hanako sneered, peering at Riley's blood-splattered naked body. "I knew you couldn't be trusted from the moment you snuck into our academy. You don't look so dangerous now, without all your ninja paraphernalia."

"Let the princess go," Riley said, glancing toward Sakura's frightened face. "All of your associates are dead. Let's settle this between the two of us."

"Whatever happened to you?" Hanako said, tightening her hold on the princess while she struggled to extricate herself. "We took you in and trained you to be an *assassin*, then you turn on your clan?"

Riley paused as she peered at Sakura with a tormented expression, nodding to indicate that everything would be okay.

"You've got to be *kidding* me," Hanako snickered, noticing the tender exchange between the two lovers. "You fell in *love* with the princess? I can't blame you, I suppose. She's pretty hot, and I know you have a thing for petite Asian girls. It'll be a shame to carve up her pretty figure, but some of us know where our allegiance lies."

"Don't do it, Hanako," Riley said. "You'll never get out of here alive. There'll be a new group of samurai guards arriving any moment, and all the other members of the royal family have already been secured."

"You know as well as I that the samurai are no match for a well-trained ninja," Hanako sneered. "And as for the rest of the royal family, there's a lot more of us waiting in the wings. It was easy enough getting into this palace and it will be just as easy for me to make my escape. Say goodbye to your little bitch."

As Hanako raised her dagger to the side of Sakura's throat, Riley peered at the princess with sad eyes, realizing that she'd be struck down long before she had a chance to get close.

15

S uddenly, Riley heard some movement behind her then an arrow flung past her body, landing with a hard thud on the floor between Hanako's parted legs.

Hanako glanced behind her, noticing Akiri standing with her bow drawn, then she shook her head.

"Seriously, Akiri?" she said. "You never were any good aiming that thing. I'll slice this girl's throat open before you have a chance to fire another arrow."

"Maybe so," Akiri nodded. "But do you want to take the chance that my next one will strike something a little softer?"

While the three girls peered at one another deciding what to do next, Sakura suddenly stomped her heel down hard on top of Hanako's slipper-bound toes, causing the larger girl to temporarily loosen her grip. Recognizing her opening, Riley reached into her bag of shuriken stars and flung one sidearm toward Hanako, catching her on the side of her chest. She yelped out in pain, and as Sakura slipped out of her grasp, Riley lunged toward Hanako, sliding across the floor as she swiped the blade of her tanto across her ankles.

Riley rose to her feet to face the taller girl with her dagger, then Hanako threw her tanto to the side, pulling her long katana from its sheath. Riley fought valiantly to defend herself against her opponent, but it soon became apparent that she was outmatched by Hanako's superior weapon. Already handicapped by her longer reach, all she could do was try to block her blows while the taller girl slowly cornered her against the window. As she crouched down closer to the floor realizing the fight would soon be over, suddenly Akiri reappeared behind her, slicing her weapon hard across Hanako's back.

Hanako swung around angrily, swinging her katana rapidly from side to side, forcing Akiri to the other side of the room while their swords slapped together loudly. When Hanako trapped her against the door frame and Akiri peered up at her with frightened eyes while she prepared to deliver the final blow, suddenly she heard a familiar voice behind her.

"Hey!" Riley yelled, grasping a shuriken star in each of her hands. "Why don't you pick on somebody your *own* size?"

Hanako paused for a moment to glance at Riley, then she snickered, stepping toward her.

"Do you really think you can stop me with those things?" she chuckled. "You obviously didn't learn the lessons of our master very well. The first rule of ninja is to recognize your limitations and select the right weapon for each battle. I'm going to slice you up like a piece of fresh sushi before I finish off your two girlfriends."

Suddenly, Akiri threw her katana toward Riley, and she

grabbed the handle with two hands, crouching into a chudan position.

"Perfect," Hanako smiled, bending down into a similar pose. "I've been waiting for this moment ever since the shihan selected you ahead of me to graduate first in our class. We'll see who's the better swordsman when the chips are down."

Hanako hesitated for a brief moment, then she lunged toward Riley, angling her sword toward her midsection. Riley blocked it easily, then she resumed her defensive pose, grinning up at Hanako.

"It should be simple for you to find plenty of open flesh to strike me this time," she smiled. "You always did like to take advantage of your opponent in their most vulnerable places. What's the matter? You can't even cut down a naked *gaikoku*?"

"I'll *cut* you alright," Hanako grunted, twisting around and slicing the tip of her sword across the side of Riley's exposed hip. "I'm going to carve you up piece by piece before I cut off your pretty head. We're not playing games any longer."

"I'm glad you noticed," Riley said, feigning to her right before swinging her sword downward and to the left, slicing a deep gash on the inside of Hanako's thigh. "You might want to have that looked at pretty soon. I might have caught your femoral artery."

Hanako glanced down at her leg gushing a torrent of blood down the inside of her thigh, then she twisted her head, noticing Sakura cowering near the corner of the four-poster bed. She lurched over toward her and grabbed her around the neck, raising her sword over her head.

"Not before I finish what I came here to do," she scowled. "If I have to go, I'm gonna take at least one of you with me."

Riley stared at Sakura with a tightened face, realizing that she was running out of options. Noticing the desperation in Hanako's eyes and realizing she could no longer escape, she had little to lose from taking the princess's life before she succumbed to her wounds. As she sneered back at Riley, Hanako pulled the princess's head back, preparing to slice open her neck with her final act.

Knowing she had to act fast, Riley lifted her katana high over her head with two hands, then she flung it end-over-end toward Hanako, striking her squarely between her eyes, pinning her head against the bedpost while Hanako stared back at her with vacant eyes.

"Riley!" Sakura said, rushing toward her lover and wrapping her arms around her waist. "Is it over?"

"Yes," Riley said, glancing toward Akiri, who was still standing by the door. "There's nobody left to hurt you now. You're safe under my protection."

Suddenly, there was a flourish of activity outside the door then the crown prince stood in the entrance with his wife and his son, surrounded by a phalanx of armed guards.

"Riley-san!" he said, peering at her naked body. "What is the meaning of this and why are you covered in blood?"

"I'm sorry, your highness," Riley said, dropping her bag of shuriken onto the floor. "I was just trying to protect you and your family..."

When the prince saw Akiri standing at the side of her door in her black ninja outfit, he ordered the guards to apprehend her.

"Wait!" Riley said, taking a step forward. "She's with me. She helped defend your daughter against these invaders."

"You *know* this woman?" the prince said, squinting his eyes at her angrily. "Who are you exactly, and why did you really come to my palace?"

"It's a long story, your majesty," Riley said, holding onto Sakura for support while she felt the wound throbbing on the side of her hip.

"Can we hold this inquisition a little *later*?" Sakura said, wrapping a bed sheet around Riley's naked body. "Right now, my friend needs some medical attention. Help me take her to the infirmary."

16

After Riley got patched up and had a chance to explain everything, the crown prince invited her and Akiri to dinner to thank them for saving the family. Riley noticed a larger than usual contingent of armed guards protecting the exits, but she knew that her ninja clan wouldn't attack the palace anytime soon, having lost the element of surprise.

"I'm not sure whether to be angry or grateful for what you've done," Prince Takayori said, peering toward Riley. "You entered the palace under false pretenses, and I fear that if you hadn't become friends with my daughter, that this could have easily gone the other way."

"Maybe so, your highness," Riley nodded. "But when I learned about your peaceful plans for ruling the country, I knew that my master was wrong about you."

"And what about your *other* friend?" the prince said, turning toward Akiri. "Has she *also* renounced her assassin's code?"

Akiri smiled while she nodded toward the prince.

"I never really signed up for this in the first place," she said. "I'm just an unassuming girl from the mountains of Tokushima. The academy was pretty much everything I knew."

"Well, it looks like you were both trained well enough to sneak into my castle and overcome my guards. Perhaps I should appoint one of *you* to be in charge of my personal security detail from now on."

"I've had enough fighting to last a lifetime, thank you very much," Riley smiled, turning toward Sakura.

"So what happens now?" the prince said. "Should we prepare for another attack by your rebel clan?"

"I can't imagine they'll be returning anytime soon," Riley nodded. "They've lost the element of surprise and seen how well defended we are."

"Does that mean you'll be staying a little longer?"

"Possibly," Riley smiled. "At least until I've fully healed. But I don't belong here. I come from a different world, and there's so much more of it to explore."

"I'll be happy to lend you one of my ships with some provisions when you're ready to leave," the prince said. "It's the least I can do for saving me and my family."

"Thank you, your highness," Riley said, nodding politely. "But I'm pretty resourceful and have my own mode of transportation. Do you mind if I take a few moments to relax now? I'm feeling exhausted after all the turmoil of the day."

"Of course," the prince said, motioning for two of his guards to escort Riley and Akiri to their rooms. "Just let me know if you need anything else."

Sakura reached under the table, clasping Riley's hand as she stood to rise.

"May I go with them, father?" she said. "I don't know how

much longer I'll have with Riley, and I feel safer under her protection anyhow."

"Yes," the prince nodded. "The guards will return their weapons and they are welcome to stay or leave their leisure."

WHILE THE THREE girls followed the guards down the hallway toward the guest quarters, Sakura thought she detected some sexual tension between Riley and Akiri, pausing outside Akiri's bed chamber.

"You two must have a lot of catching up to do," she said, peering at Riley. "Why don't you join me later, after you've fully recovered?"

Riley glanced at Akiri then she turned to smile at Sakura.

"I have to confess that I fibbed a little bit with your father over dinner," she said. "I'm not really feeling tired at all. I just wanted to have some alone time with the two of you before we got separated again."

"Well if it's *sex* you're hungry for," the princess said, feeling a tinge of jealousy. "Perhaps you should take one course at a time. I'll be waiting for you in my chambers when you're done here."

But as she turned to leave, Riley reached out and grabbed her hand.

"Why not join the two of us right now?" Riley smiled. "Sex between women is even more fun when there's *three* of us together."

"Really?" Sakura said, widening her eyes. "I couldn't even imagine..."

"There's no need to fantasize any longer," Riley grinned,

pulling the two girls toward the bed. Let me show you something the French discovered a long time ago..."

THE THREE WOMEN made love into the wee hours, then Riley lay awake in the bed surrounded by her lovers while they slept peacefully. Sensing that her work in Japan was done, she crept out of bed and removed her small time machine from the inside pocket of her kimono. Tapping the front of the screen, the device whirred to life, illuminating the room with the 3-D funnel rising over the glass. As Riley lifted her arm to the edge of the vortex, she felt her body slowly being pulled inside, and she glanced at her two lovers lying quietly on the bed.

"Riley?" the princess said, sitting up when she noticed the strange apparition rising out of the palm of her hands. "What is that thing–?"

"I'm sorry, Sakura," Riley said, peering back at the princess with a tear rolling down the front of her cheek. "I have to leave now. But I'll never forget the time we've had together..."

As her body began to disappear into the swirling cloud, both of the girls leapt off the bed, but it was too late. Riley felt herself tumbling through the time machine portal once again, wondering where she'd land this time. After a few minutes, she plopped down on a dusty courtyard surrounded by stone houses with tiled roofs. While she struggled to raise herself up on her arms, she was surrounded by a trio of armed soldiers wearing metal helmets and brass chestplates. Glancing around her surroundings, she noticed tall mountains rising up on every side.

"What now?" she thought, peering at the pointed spears of the puzzled soldiers. "And why can't I ever land somewhere quiet and peaceful?"

READY FOR MORE STEAMY ADVENTURES? Order the next exciting volume in Riley's Time Travel Adventures:

The battle that changed the face of Western Civilization...

ALSO BY VICTORIA RUSH

Wet your whistle a hundred different ways with Jade's Erotic Adventures. Browse the full collection of Victoria Rush steamy stories here:

Click to scan your favorites...

FOLLOW VICTORIA RUSH:

Want to keep informed of my latest erotic book releases? Sign up for my newsletter and receive a FREE bonus book:

Spying on the neighbors just got a lot more interesting...

Lightning Source UK Ltd.
Milton Keynes UK
UKHW040822020123
414708UK00004B/381

9 798215 736555